RUBY AND THE PARCEL BEAR

Maggie Glen

RED FOX

For Lucy and Lily

A Red Fox Book

Published by Random House Children's Books
20 Vauxhall Bridge Road, London SW1V 2SA

A division of Random House UK Ltd
London Melbourne Sydney Auckland
Johannesburg and agencies throughout the world

1 3 5 7 9 10 8 6 4 2

First published in Great Britain by Hutchinson Children's Books 1995

Red Fox edition 1999

Printed in Hong Kong

RANDOM HOUSE UK Limited Reg. No. 954009

ISBN 0 091 87299 5

‘Wow, I just can’t believe it,’ Ruby gasped as she saw all the presents. ‘It must be my birthday.’

Ruby, Susie and Susie’s mum were staying with Auntie Rose.

One parcel looked very different from the others. It was much bigger and a very strange shape.

Just a little hole won't show, she thought as she started to pick at the paper.

Suddenly the parcel started to move; then it rustled and wiggled, then...

It GROWLED!

'Stop that!' said the parcel. 'It tickles.'

Ruby jumped. 'What on earth *is* it?' she said as she saw a furry paw emerge from the paper.

'Stop it!' said the voice again.

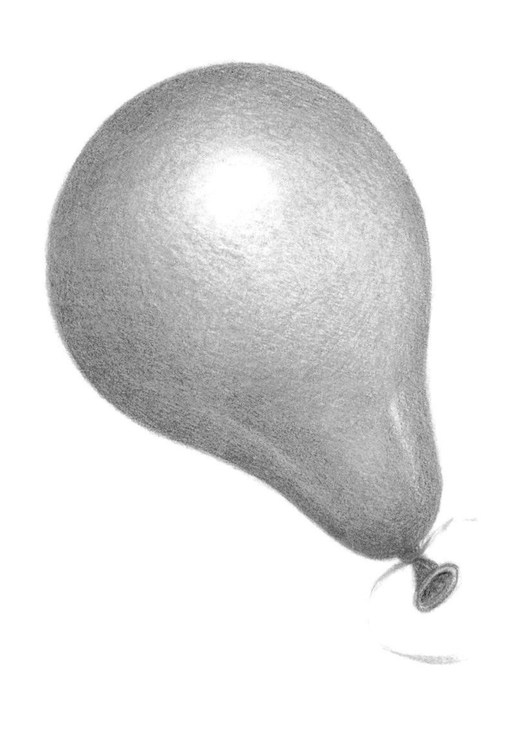

But Ruby couldn't stop; she was far too excited. She picked a bigger hole and saw an eye staring at her.

'You're another bear,' she gasped.

'Of course I am,' the parcel bear growled. 'But you shouldn't be picking at the paper. These presents are not for you.'

'What, none of them?' Ruby gasped. 'Not even the tiny one?'

'No, it's Susie's birthday, not yours. I'm her new bear, Albert, and I'm a particularly fine bear. All the best kinds of bears come in parcels.'

'But I didn't come in a parcel,' said Ruby quietly.

'Quite so,' replied Albert, before Ruby had a chance to say that she was special too.

'Anyway,' said Ruby, *'I'm* Susie's bear, so there must be some mistake.'

Albert looked at Ruby. He stared at her spotty tummy.

'You're the mistake,' he said. 'I'm the proper bear.'

T H D A Y

Suddenly, both bears were startled as the door burst open and in rushed Susie, followed by her cousins, Millie and Charlie. Everyone was singing 'Happy Birthday'.

Ruby felt a little more cheerful. Staying at Auntie Rose's was always fun.

'Someone's been peeking at the parcels,' laughed Auntie Rose, as Susie opened her presents.

'Look, Ruby,' cried Susie as she unwrapped Albert. 'Another bear. Isn't he wonderful? You can be friends.'

Now that Ruby could see the whole of Albert, she didn't like the look of him at all. He was very new and smart and had a snooty look on his face.

Later, at teatime, Susie sat Albert on her lap and put Ruby beside her on the chair.

Ruby glared at Albert; how dare he sit in her place!

Just then, Susie leaned over the table to blow out the candles. She forgot all about Albert sitting on her lap.

Splat! He landed face-down in the trifle.

Everyone laughed.

Albert didn't like being laughed at. He looked accusingly at Ruby.

'You pushed me!' he hissed. 'Still, I don't suppose you can expect a spotty bear to have any manners.'

'But I didn't,' protested Ruby.

Albert had to have his face wiped with a dishcloth.

Serves you right, thought Ruby.

Susie felt very sorry that she had let Albert fall in the trifle, so she played with him for the rest of the day.

She brushed his fur and tied and untied his ribbon.

She tucked him up in the toy bed and told him lots of stories.

Albert smiled sweetly. He looked across at Ruby as if to say, 'I'm Susie's bear now.'

The next day Susie and her mum packed up their things and got ready to leave.

'Hurry, or you'll miss the train,' Auntie Rose called up the stairs. 'If you forget anything, I'll post it on.'

Ruby listened. *Post it on,* she thought. That means in a parcel.

Then quickly as she could, she rolled out of the basket and under the bed. She held her breath until she heard the front door close.

As she turned round she saw a pair of bright eyes looking at her.

'Oh, hello,' said Ruby to the little cat. 'What are you doing here?'

'I'm stuck,' he replied. 'One of the children hid me under the mattress and forgot all about me.'

'I'm *hiding*,' said Ruby, 'because I want to be missed. When Auntie Rose finds me I'll be sent home in a parcel. All the best kinds of bears come in parcels.'

'Well, I've been here for weeks and weeks,' said the cat, 'and no one's missed me.'

Ruby began to worry.

She was just about to help the little cat get unstuck when she heard a terrifying noise.

Whoosh! Ruby clung to the leg of the bed as she felt herself being pulled hard by her left foot.

'Ruby!' cried Auntie Rose. 'How on earth did you get under there? And look, there's Kitty too.'

Auntie Rose put Kitty away in the toy basket.

Then she sat Ruby on her knees.

'I suppose I'd better send you home,' she said. 'But first I'll knit you a snug new jumper to keep you warm on the journey.'

When the jumper was finished she put Ruby in a parcel with some other things that Susie had forgotten.

Then she took it to the Post Office.

'I'd like to send this parcel Special Delivery, please,' Auntie Rose said.

Royal Mail
SPECIAL Delivery
5:15 PM
£1
CARRICKFERGUS CASTLE
£1
CARRICKFERGUS CASTLE
Miss Susie Robertson,
143, Ferndale Road,
LOUGHBOROUGH
Leicestershire
LE11 2YP

Inside the parcel it was very dark and frightening. Head over heels, heels over head Ruby went, tumbling and sliding about in the box.

'Are we nearly there yet?' she shouted crossly.

But no one heard.

At last the van stopped. Ruby heard the door open and someone picked her up.

Tuesday
Dear Susie,
It was so lovely to
see you and for your

Then there were footsteps followed by a sound she knew well. Ding-dong.

Susie rushed into the hall as her grandad took the parcel from the postman.

'It's for you, Susie,' he said. 'I think it might be from Auntie Rose.'

Susie held her breath as she started to unwrap the parcel.

'Oh, I hope it's...

RUBY!'

Susie hugged her tight.

'Albert is a nice bear,' she said, 'but I've really missed you.'

'And so have I,' mumbled a deep voice nearby. 'It's been rather quiet on my own.'

Susie, Ruby and Albert shared a welcome-home tea. This time Ruby sat on Susie's lap.

'You came in a parcel,' said Albert thoughtfully, 'so I suppose you must be a proper bear after all.'

'Of course I am,' Ruby said proudly. 'Special Delivery!'